Simon Mole Sam

I love my CAT

Frances Lincoln
Children's Books

I love my cat.

That shiny black fur.

That tiny white ring,

that goes right round the tip of her tail,

I think it means she might be magic!

When she nudges and nuzzles

her head against my leg,

I know she loves me back.

I love my cat.

The way she

leaps up

and pushes

with her paw

at my bedroom

door handle.

My cat can open doors!

She taught herself to turn the tap on.

She can drink from the sink!

And if you say, "Hello, Aditi,"
and then look at her,
I mean really look at her,
sometimes she miaows *right back.*
It's like we have a chat.

"Addie-Addie-Adster!"

I love my cat!

Dad says Aditi *means freedom.*

Mostly we call her Addie, or Dozey Dee-Dee.

Or if she's being grumpy we say, "Ada-saurus Rex."

She really is a big, big *sleeper.*

All curled up.

All day long.

Mum calls her a lazybones*, but I think Addie's got the right idea.*

Nobody wakes her *up for school*

or *tells her to stay in bed longer*

at the weekend . . .

How can she be a lazybones anyway?

I've seen what she can do when she wants *to . . .*

Helping Mum to tie her shoelace.

Giving Dad a hand to change the duvet.

Or bringing little presents *in to pack inside my suitcase.*

I've even seen
my little Addie-Boos
run up a wall.

Up a wall!

Perhaps she is magic after all!

And anytime I'm watching telly with a snack,

quick as a flash,

Addie's up there on my lap.

"PURR!

PURRR!

PURRRRRRRRRRR!"

And I love my cat.

But

when she tries

to nibble

at my toast . . .

And won't give up.

And won't give up

and . . .

. . . **still** *won't give up*

and digs her claws in,

so there's no way

I can

stop

us both

from

falling,

I shout,

today I really, really shout,

"NOT AGAIN, ADDIE!

OUT! OUT! OUT!"

Tonight when we called her in for dinner
Addie didn't come.
Even when we bang-a-langed *her bowl*
from the balcony.

"Aditi!

Aditi-feetie!

Sweetie!

Dozy Dee-Dee!

Din-Dins!"

She still wasn't back by the time I went to bed.

Wasn't back when I got up in the night
to check with Dad.

Wasn't even back in the morning for breakfast.
Just looking at my slice of toast
made me feel bad.

All I could think about
at school all day was Addie.

And when Dad picked me up,
I could tell straight away from the look on his face.

She was still missing.

On the way home
we knocked on every *door in our street.*

We searched all *of the sheds*

on the allotment.

Plant pots,

wheel barrows,

compost bins . . .

But there was no sign of Addie.

What if she's upset
about me shouting?

After tea I made thirteen LOST CAT posters.

Dad said some people thought thirteen was an unlucky number,
so I scrunched one of the posters up,
squishing it and squashing it again and again,
and then I started crying as I dropped it in the bin.

I didn't even care
about the numbers really.
I just wanted
my little Addie Boo-Boos to be safe.

Dad said we didn't know for sure
that Addie was in trouble.
"Remember what Aditi means?" I didn't.

"Freedom!"

"Cats aren't like us," he said.
"They don't leave notes or make plans.
They just go out when they want to.
And come back when they're ready."

Maybe Addie isn't stuck in a shed after all.

Maybe she met some cat friends

and one of them said, "Hey!

Let's go back to mine for a party!"

Maybe Addie's at an awesome cat party right now.

Or it could be that she really is magic and
she's travelled back in time to ancient Egypt!

They treated cats like kings and queens so . . .
Addie could be in a sparkly cat crown now,
being fed a banquet of delicious fancy treats,
in a massive palace so much bigger than our flat.

If she really is magic maybe she can hear me thinking,

I miss my cat.
Addie, please come back!

A week later and
the posters we had put up
weren't looking so good.

Every little scratch
or bump I hear,
I think it's her.

But it's making me so tired
that I'm trying to train my brain to ignore the sort of sounds

that might be her . . .

But won't be her.

Like that silly scritchy-scratching that will stop soon.

Scritchy.

Scratch.

Hold on, it hasn't stopped . . .

"Dad,
what's that?"

Two pointy ears.

That shiny black fur! Is it her?

That tiny white ring

that goes right round the tip of her tail.

Am I dreaming? Is this magic?

Then she nudges and nuzzles her head against my neck.

And I know she's **really** *back!*

"Addie-Baddie-Boo-Boos!"

I love my cat.

Before I sit down on the sofa,
this time I get us both *a snack.*

“Addie-Baddie-Boo-Boos!”

I love my cat.

For all the young poets out there,
especially the absolute legends at my online
workshops – keep writing! — Simon

For Sebastian — Sam

Brimming with creative inspiration, how-to projects, and useful information to enrich your everyday life, quarto.com is a favourite destination for those pursuing their interests and passions.

First published in 2022 by Frances Lincoln Children's Books, an imprint of The Quarto Group.
The Old Brewery, 6 Blundell Street, London N7 9BH, United Kingdom.
T (0)20 7700 6700 F (0)20 7700 8066 www.Quarto.com

A catalogue record for this book is available from the British Library.

ISBN 978-0-7112-7651-2

The illustrations were created in watercolour
Set in Woodford Bourne Pro

Published and edited by Peter Marley
Designed by Sarah Malley
Production by Dawn Cameron

Manufactured in Guangdong, China TT042022
10 9 8 7 6 5 4 3 2 1